Crossbow

D0188219

Dayle Campbell Gaetz

Orca currents

ORCA BOOK PUBLISHERS

Library and Archives Canada Cataloguing in Publication

Gaetz, Dayle, 1947-

Crossbow / written by Dayle Campbell Gaetz

(Orca currents)

ISBN 978-1-55143-843-6 (bound)

ISBN 978-1-155143-841-2 (pbk.)

I. Title. II. Series.

PS8563A25317C76 2007   jC813'.54   C2007-903834-4

Summary: Matt needs more than a crossbow to survive.

First published in the United States, 2007
Library of Congress Control Number: 2007930415

Orca Book Publishers gratefully acknowledges the support for its publishing
programs provided by the following agencies: the Government of Canada
through the Book Publishing Industry Development Program and the
Canada Council for the Arts, and the Province of British Columbia
through the BC Arts Council and the Book Publishing Tax Credit.

Cover design: Teresa Bubela
Cover photography: Masterfile

Orca Book Publishers
PO Box 5626, Station B
Victoria, BC Canada
V8R 6S4

Orca Book Publishers
PO Box 468
Custer, WA USA
98240-0468

www.orcabook.com
Printed and bound in Canada.
Printed on 100% PCW recycled paper.

010 09 08 07 • 4 3 2 1

For Russ, born outdoorsman and builder of cabins in the woods.

chapter one

I was a cougar slinking through the forest. Silent. Unseen. Bushes parted to let me pass and closed behind me like lacy green curtains. I marched uphill with long even strides, my feet as soundless as a big cat's paws on the forest floor.

Massive tree trunks soared from the thick undergrowth like a thousand giant pillars. High above my head their branches hid the sky. This was where I belonged.

No one could bother me here. Trees never whispered behind my back.

I felt light and free, like an escaped prisoner. Tonight, for the first time ever, I would sleep up here on my own. Just me and the wilderness. I wanted to bellow out in triumph, like a big old bull elk. But I had almost reached my cabin, so I loped along on silent feet. Like a creature of the wild, I approached my lair in silence. I slowed down, advanced cautiously, stayed on high alert to keep my territory safe from predators.

I raised my head, sniffed the air and knew something was wrong. Mixed with the musty odor of damp earth and the Christmas-tree scent of firs, was a trace of wood smoke. A chill spread up the back of my neck. Here in the forest, smoke could come from only one place. My cabin. Someone must be there. I stopped and peered through a veil of green branches, listening hard. Then I smiled grimly.

Stop. Look. Listen. That's what they teach you in kindergarten. Good advice.

It's the most important thing I ever learned at school. They forgot *smell*, though. *Stop. Look. Listen. Smell*. The smoke smell was stronger now and mixed with an enticing aroma. Meat. Someone was cooking meat. It smelled so good I started to drool.

Nothing looked out of place. Gray strands of mist floated around the tree branches and masked any smoky haze. The only sound was constant drip-drip-dripping of water from mist-wet trees. Then, so close I jumped, I heard a soft growl. I held my breath, strained to hear. The growl came again, louder, closer than before.

A grin crept across my face, and I pressed my hand against my stomach. What a dope! The growls came from my own empty belly. My grin froze when I heard the clunk. The thud of an axe striking a chunk of wood. My wood.

Someone had found my cabin. But who? How? I had always been so careful. I built it miles back in the forest where no one would ever find it. But someone had, so what was I going to do about it?

Decision time. I couldn't hide in the bushes all night. I had two choices. I could slink away and pretend I'd never been here or I could confront the guy. My heart pounded in my ears. I turned away.

The next thud was followed by the shriek of wood splitting apart. Light dry kindling bounced and clattered against stone. The stone by my door, next to my fire pit. Fear burned into anger. Keeping low, hidden by thick brush, I crept forward. I reached a young cedar near the side of my cabin and hid behind its low branches.

Only a small part of one wall showed through the low-hanging branches. The logs, about five inches across, were sealed together with thick clay-like mud. The logs came from a clear-cut nearby. They were the wrong species, or too small, or too crooked, so the logging company that mowed them down had left them to rot. Only the perfect ones were worth keeping. Kind of like kids— if you weren't perfect you got left behind.

I had started building my cabin in July, after my father was gone. I borrowed his chainsaw. He wouldn't need it for a long time. I chose the best of the junk trees, cut off their branches and chopped them into ten-foot lengths. I hauled them, one at a time, to my site. The job took all summer and into the fall, but it was worth all that hard work to have a place of my own. A place to be alone.

Since my main ambition in life was to be a hermit, I figured it was time to get some work experience. My mom said I should work hard at school, but she didn't understand the importance of on-the-job training. She didn't understand why this cabin was so important to me either. I brought her up here when it was almost finished. She looked at the four square walls, the tarpaper roof, my little plastic-covered window and the old door I dragged up from home.

"It's a nice fort," she had said.

Like I was some little kid, playing games.

My attention swung back to a fire that crackled in my fire pit. Above the fire, on a tripod made of stout green sticks, hung a chunk of meat big enough to feed ten people. It looked like a roast beef, sizzling over the flames. A tempting aroma drifted through the bushes and reminded me of my grandma's kitchen on a Sunday evening.

My stomach churned, the smell of cooking meat sickened me now. I held my breath and tried not to think about the good old days, before the accident. I hadn't tasted roast beef since then.

I carefully slid my backpack from one arm and then the other, lowering it to the thick carpet of brown fir needles. I had formed a plan, but I didn't want the back-pack slowing me down if I needed to run.

chapter two

I heard him before I saw him. He was just whistling some tune from ancient history, an old song that reminded me of my father. I felt like throttling him. Two black hiking boots stopped near the fire, legs as solid as tree trunks, arms loaded with wood. My wood. Wood he had chopped with my axe. Anger rose in my throat. How could I not be mad? This guy came from nowhere and took over my cabin. I clenched my teeth and tried to ignore his disgusting whistling.

I searched the ground for a strong stick, found a good solid one and crouched behind the tree. I waited for him to turn his back.

No luck. Still facing my hiding spot, he let his bundle of wood clatter to the ground near his boots. He bent to pick up one good-sized piece, then another, and then he placed them on the fire.

I wasn't stupid enough to race out there and tackle him. He looked big. Well, okay, he was no football player, but he was bigger than me. In a year or two I could take him, but at fourteen I still had some growing to do.

He looked about six feet tall and was built like a truck. He had wide shoulders under his green camo shirt. His pants were hitched up with dirty red suspenders. No joke, real suspenders! Like Santa Claus. When you have a potbelly like Santa Claus you need more than a belt to hold your pants up. But this guy didn't have a potbelly, he was a lean, mean fighting machine. His scraggly brown beard matched the long stringy hair that stuck out below his hunting cap. The cap was bright orange and had wide earflaps.

The guy had to be out of his mind. What kind of idiot wore camouflage topped off with red suspenders and an orange hunting cap? Like a chameleon wearing a bright red ribbon.

He picked up a long piece of wood and poked the fire, sending up a shower of sparks. Then he reached over the fire and stuck his finger on the meat. He raised the finger to his mouth, tasted it and licked his lips.

My mouth watered. The revulsion I had felt was pushed away by hunger. My knees ached from crouching for too long. I shifted my weight, wishing I could stand up and stretch my legs. When I looked back, the guy was staring right at me.

He couldn't see me. That's what I told myself anyway. I was hidden in thick bush behind the cedar. My dark jacket and pants blended in with the late afternoon shadows. I took quick shallow breaths and clutched the heavy stick like a club.

The man looked away. He laid his piece of wood on top of the fire. Then he stood and walked toward the cabin door, out of sight from my hiding spot.

So, now what was I supposed to do? My only chance was to take him by surprise. Sneak up behind and gonk him on the head. But could I do it? Did I want to? Maybe he was lost. Maybe he was following the code of the bush: *If you're lost or hungry and need shelter for the night, any cabin is open to you.*

Before I could decide what to do, he was back. This time he carried a couple of tin plates with something on them, maybe potatoes or onions, I couldn't quite see. He moved around the fire and crouched with his back to me. One at a time he placed the items from the plates onto the hot coals.

This was my chance. I could run forward and smack him right on top of that orange hunting cap. With any luck he would fall forward into the fire. And then what? I'd be stuck up here with a stranger who had a burned face and a bad headache. What was I supposed to do with him then?

Besides, what chance did I have to take him by surprise? I needed to get through these thick bushes and gonk him hard before he heard a thing. Impossible. I had the feeling this man knew what he was doing. He looked as wary as a wolf.

I should just leave. First chance I got I would creep away, grab my pack and head home. Tomorrow I would come back and hope he was gone.

"This your cabin?"

The voice came from nowhere and everywhere at once. It rose out of the mist and floated down from the trees. I froze, my heart pounding, and stared down at the club in my hand. It looked useless now. Feeble. The fire crackled cheerfully in front of me. Behind me the forest hung silent and cold.

The stranger stood up. He turned toward my hiding place. His pale eyes seemed to bore right into mine. "I asked you a question, boy. Is this your cabin?"

My eyes fell to his black boots. I swallowed and knew I couldn't speak. You can't speak when your throat seizes up so bad you can barely breathe. How did he know I was here? Did he hear the leaves rustle when I shifted position? Even then, how could he know I was a boy? He couldn't see me, I was sure of that. So I could be anything—a bird, a cougar, a man.

"You may as well come out." He didn't move, he simply stood there, waiting.

My eyes rolled up to his face again. He was looking right at me and smiling. "Dinner's almost ready," he said as if he'd been expecting me all along.

chapter three

I pushed myself awkwardly to my feet. A cedar branch brushed the back of my neck and sent a shiver of cold water down my spine. I pressed forward, pushing branches aside, ducking under the thick foliage.

The man reached out to hold back a curtain of dark green. "Come on in," he smiled like he was greeting me at his front door.

But it wasn't a door, and it sure wasn't his. "What are you doing in my cabin?" I growled.

He dropped his arm and stepped back, looking surprised and hurt. "I'm sorry, but I didn't think you'd mind. It's so wet out here, and I had nowhere else to go."

I nodded. The code of the bush. "So, you're staying here all night?"

"If that's okay with you."

I shrugged and pushed past him to the fire. I laid the stick near my feet and stretched my hands over the hot flames.

"Because, if you want me to go I'll leave right now." He moved to the far side of the fire, where he could see my face. But I refused to look up.

This was where I was supposed to say something like, No, please stay, you can't sleep out in the rain all night. But I didn't want him here. This was my first night in the cabin after all that hard work, and I wanted to be alone. I stared into the leaping orange flames where a pair of fat potatoes and two round onions roasted on glowing coals. The roast sizzled and spit fat into the flames, making them flare up. It smelled awesome.

"I'll even leave you my venison. It's almost done," he said.

"No," I heard myself say, "that wouldn't be fair. It's your meat."

"It's your cabin."

I looked across the fire at him. Warm light flickered across his face. The bright orange peak of his hunting cap glowed and his pale eyes glimmered. He watched me, his mouth open only a slit, waiting for my answer as if his life depended on my decision. But would he really leave if I asked him to?

Crunch time. If I told him to go he might get angry and tell me to take off. On the other hand, he might simply leave. I had to know. "You're right," I told him. "This is my cabin and you have no business being here." I glared at him, while the fire burned hot on my face. At the first sign of anger from him I was ready to bolt, but I didn't move a muscle. I kept a fierce look on my face, while my heart pounded in my ears.

His shoulders slumped. "Fine, I understand," he said. "You must be planning to sleep here tonight?"

My fierce look slipped a little. I hadn't expected another question. What I wanted was a clear answer, either he'd stay or pack up and go. Why did he care if I was staying here all night?

It hit me then that he could be a deranged killer on the loose. I mean, who knew where he came from? So I shook my head. "No, I told my mom I was only going to check on the cabin. She's expecting me back soon."

He nodded, rubbed his hands over the fire and said, "All right then, I'll clear out of here." He reached up to pull the orange earflaps over his ears and turned toward the cabin.

"Wait!" I called. "You may as well eat your dinner first, after all it is your food."

He turned back. A wide grin split his face. In spite of his beard, his stringy hair and a black smudge across one cheek, there was something appealing about his face. He had a thoughtful look about him, as if he knew a whole lot about life.

The thing that got me though, was the way he waited for me to speak as if my opinion mattered. As if we were equals. My father used to treat me like that before everything fell apart.

"Can you join me for dinner?" he asked. "Or will your mom call out a search party?"

I laughed. "She'll be okay for an hour or two."

"Good, then it's settled. Want to turn those potatoes and onions over? I'll get a couple of mugs for the coffee."

That's when I noticed the blackened coffee pot perched on a rock up close to the fire. A trickle of steam puffed from its spout. As I bent to turn the vegetables a whiff of coffee assaulted my nostrils. And I do mean assaulted. I never much liked coffee, but when Mom made it at home it always smelled wonderful. This stuff smelled like burnt grease. It smelled like a stomachache.

By then the man was walking back from the cabin with my mug and a tin cup that must have been his. Without asking if I wanted any, he filled both mugs. "I hope you don't take cream and sugar," he said as he handed me my mug, "because you'd be out of luck."

I shook my head. "This is fine." I gazed down at the black goop that filled the chipped white mug I had brought from home. I wrapped my hands around its warmth and tried to prepare my stomach for the onslaught.

"People call me Forrest." He perched on a short cedar log and raised his mug with both hands. He took a sip, shuddered and took another one. "Ah," he said, "now that's coffee."

"I'm Matthew." I settled on a log. I raised my mug, sniffed the coffee and quickly lowered it again. "How did you know I was here?"

"Simple. I heard you rattling through the bushes," he said.

"But I was being quiet!"

"Quieter than most. Not so quiet as you might think."

"I suppose you can do better?" I asked.

He shrugged. "I've had more practice."

"So, how come you stared right at me?" I asked. "You couldn't see me."

He sipped his coffee, didn't answer.

"Could you?"

"What?" he asked.

"See me?"

"Nah, not exactly," he said. "Heard you breathing, though. Saw your breath too. No one takes Forrest by surprise."

I stared at him. A trail of vapor curled up from his coffee, as did a puff of moist air from his nostrils. But I had been hidden by cedar branches. Or not. This guy was good.

chapter four

When the venison was done, Forrest cut off a thick slab and slapped it on a tin plate. He grabbed a charcoal potato and a black ball of an onion from the fire, tossed them on top and handed the plate to me. The meat was crisp black on the outside and juicy pink in the middle.

I sawed through a quarter inch of hard black crust around my potato. Inside it was so soft and fluffy it tasted great, even without butter or salt. The onion wasn't bad either, filled with squishy tender layers. The charcoal added a flavor of its own.

But the roast. Oh, man! Maybe not so tender as Grandma used to cook, but it had a wild, exciting taste that I loved. I gobbled everything down in record time and swallowed half of that disgusting coffee along with it. "Man, was that good! Thanks, Forrest."

"No." He shook his head. "I thank you for letting me stay." He glanced above the treetops at a slate gray sky, and then he stood up and reached for my plate. "I'm afraid I have to eat and run. I need to find a place to sleep before the night turns as black as my cooking."

He laughed, but I felt terrible. Was this really what I wanted? How could I sleep all nice and dry inside the cabin if he was out in the cold damp forest? But I couldn't stay here with him either; that would be stupid. I didn't even know the guy. I needed time to sort out my thoughts, so I asked, "Where'd you get the venison?"

He gestured with his head. "I picked up a buck near the lake."

"You have a gun?"

"Nah. Never owned a gun. Messy, noisy things. Besides, I figure the animal deserves a fighting chance. Use a gun and they're dead before you get anywhere near."

"So, how'd you get the deer?" I asked.

"Wait right there and I'll show you."

Carrying the two plates and the last of the venison, Forrest trudged toward my cabin door. He came back with something under his arm. It was odd looking, like a rifle with an archery bow attached sideways on the front.

"What is that, a crossbow?" I asked.

He nodded.

My heart did a little flip-flop when I noticed the arrow set in place. He raised the crossbow and before I could react, he aimed and pulled the trigger. The arrow whooshed past my ear and slammed into the trunk of the cedar tree where I had been hiding earlier. The hairs on my neck stood on end.

He lowered the crossbow. "It's very accurate," he said.

My jaw hung open so wide I almost choked. If he had aimed that thing at me—but of course he hadn't. I pushed my mouth closed with the back of my hand. "Awesome," I whispered.

"It's not hard, just takes a little practice."

I studied the cedar tree. Its branches formed a thick blanket, and there was no sign of the arrow. "When I was hiding in there, how did you know I wasn't a cougar or maybe a man?"

"Simple. You made too much noise for a cougar and I saw your stuff inside. I admire how you built this cabin, Matthew. You did a better job than me when I was your age."

"You built a cabin too?"

He nodded. "Not near as fancy as yours. My dad called it a fort."

"That's what my mom said when she saw it," I said.

He pushed his hunting cap back from his forehead. "What about your dad?"

His question slammed into my stomach. Sounds screeched inside my head. I gazed up at the quiet trees and took a deep breath, struggling for control.

After a minute Forrest muttered, "I'll get the rest of my gear and clear out of here."

I watched Forrest's retreating back and suddenly wanted to be home. "No, wait! I need to go anyway. You might as well sleep here tonight."

He turned and nodded. "I appreciate that, Matt. Mind if I call you Matt? Matthew sounds a bit stuffy, don't you think?"

I thought of the way my mother refused to let anyone, ever, call me Matt. "Sounds good to me."

It's a good thing I knew the trail so well, otherwise I might have gotten lost on my way home. Darkness closes in early by late October, especially on a gloomy evening where tall trees block out most of the light.

By the time I reached our small town at the edge of the lake, rain was teaming down. Lights from the houses cast bleary reflections on the wet pavement. The pulp mill at the edge of town was a black hulk, no lights, no stinky smell.

No jobs. If my dad was still working at the mill, maybe he wouldn't have started drinking, maybe none of the bad stuff would have happened. I kept my head down and hurried home. By the back door I yanked off my muddy boots. "Mom?" I called, "I'm home."

She hurried to meet me, a book in one hand and surprise all over her face. "Matthew! Are you okay? I thought you were staying in your fort all night. What happened?"

I cringed at the word *fort*. "I changed my mind. It's was uh...kinda cold up there at my cabin."

She smiled and placed her hand on my shoulder. "I'm glad you're back, Matthew. I wouldn't have slept a wink thinking of you all alone up there!"

"How about hot chocolate?" I suggested. "I'll make it."

"Sounds good to me."

chapter five

Mom sat on a kitchen stool and curled her fingers around her hot chocolate. "Did you hear about the break-in?" she asked.

I raised my hot chocolate and drank. Its rich warmth filled my mouth and wiped out the last memory of Forrest's bitter coffee. I scooped up some fluffy, sweet, whipped cream on my tongue. At the same time, I watched Mom and wondered if she was losing it. Didn't we talk about the break-in already?

She must have guessed what I was thinking because she added, "I don't mean the one last week, Matthew, there's been another one. This time it was the McNair's summer cabin down by the lake. Luckily they came up for the weekend or they might not have known for weeks."

"So? When did it happen?"

"They figure it was yesterday, after the rain started. There were muddy prints just inside the door, but it seems the thief took off his boots so he wouldn't make a mess!"

"Very considerate," I said.

"He didn't do any damage either. Somehow he opened the door without breaking the lock. The police say he knew what he was doing, so he's most likely a professional thief."

"Who knew thieving was a profession?" I grinned. "It makes being a hermit sound a whole lot better, doesn't it?"

Mom's faced turned sad. "Matthew..."

"So?" I cut her off. "What did he take?"

"The police won't say exactly, but I know there was food missing from the freezer and some of Tom McNair's clothes were gone. The thief didn't take anything valuable, even though some brand-new stereo equipment was in plain view."

"A professional crook who only steals food and secondhand clothes? He should go back to Crook College for a refresher course."

Mom laughed.

The next morning I dragged myself out of bed and looked out the window. A weak sun was pushing through the mist that rolled in off the lake. I stumbled into the kitchen where Mom was drinking coffee and drawing circles around ads in the newspaper.

She looked up. "Want to come saling with me?"

I yawned. "Garage saling? No thanks, I'd rather go for a hike."

Her smile shriveled. "Not up to your fort again?"

"It's not a fort," I snapped. "It's a cabin. And why shouldn't I go there?"

She looked hurt, which made me feel bad. Why didn't she just get mad and yell like other parents do? "Matthew, it's not good to be alone so much. Ever since..." She looked up at me.

I held my breath, waiting, wanting to cover my ears with my hands. Was she going to talk about what my father did?

She bit her lip and circled another ad. "You never hang out with friends anymore. Why don't you phone Amanda? You two always got along so well, and she loves the outdoors as much as you do."

"Mom," I tried to explain, "Amanda and I played together when we were little kids. We haven't been friends for years. Besides, she plays soccer on Saturdays."

"Okay then, there's Tyler. You like him, don't you?"

I shrugged. "Sure, he's okay. But you'll never catch him hiking in the woods. He'd rather be at the mall."

Mom tapped her pen on the table. "Matthew, you know I don't like it when you wander into the woods alone."

"Trust me, Mom, I know what I'm doing. Besides, it's part of my work experience."

She put down the pen. "Oh, Matthew, not that hermit thing again?"

I grinned. "Hey, how many fourteen-year-old guys have a long-term career goal in mind?"

She pressed both hands to her forehead as if it hurt. "Being a hermit is not a career goal."

"No," I agreed, "it's a way of life. I like being alone, I like the wilderness and I don't much like people. Being a hermit is my calling."

Mom sighed and got up from the table. We'd had this argument before and would have it again. Right now, she needed to get going. She'd gone to garage sales every Saturday morning for as long as I could remember. The good news was she didn't drag me along anymore.

After Mom left I got my backpack and carried it to the kitchen. I took the butter from the fridge, sliced off a big chunk and wrapped it up. I poured cream into a plastic water bottle and sugar into a small jar. I tossed in a loaf of bread, two cans of chicken soup and a box of crackers. I thought for a second and then went back to the fridge for a hunk of cheese and a couple of apples. Finally I grabbed my jacket and headed outside.

Amanda was standing at the end of her driveway. Her head swung toward me and her short brown curls fluttered around her freckled face. "Want to come and watch my game?" she asked. "Brianna's mom could give you a ride."

"Thanks, but nope. You know I'm not into sports, Amanda, but I hope you have fun."

"I will." Her dark brown eyes stared straight into mine, from exactly the same height. In her shiny blue soccer jacket and black shorts she looked strong and fit. Amanda had been able to out-run me, out-swim me and beat me at anything else that resembles sports since we were three years old. Her eyes wandered to my pack. "Where are you going with that fat backpack?"

"Nowhere," I snapped. I had never told Amanda about my cabin. Once, in the summer when I was building it, I almost told her but I chickened out. She would never understand. What if she laughed at me and told her friends about Matthew and his fort?

"Sorry I asked," she said. Her angry eyes looked past me, up the street.

Why do I always say the wrong thing and make people mad at me? I tried again. "It's no big deal. I'm just going for a hike, nowhere special." I patted the strap of my pack. "I like to be prepared in case I get lost or something."

A blue minivan stopped in front of us. "Here's my ride," she said. She hopped in and slammed the door shut. Which is impressive since the door was a slider.

chapter six

Once more a creature of the wild, I stopped, looked and listened. Nothing. I sniffed the air and crept forward. Slowly, slowly, one foot down, shift weight, move other foot, silent as the mist. Forrest wouldn't hear a thing. How could he? I couldn't even hear myself.

There was no hint of smoke. Was he still asleep? A breath of wind swished through the trees overhead, and then the silence returned. I moved on, soundless as the forest, hunched forward, on silent feet. I circled to the sloping ground above my cabin where I had dragged all the logs down from the clear-cut. That left a wide swath where the bushes were trampled and sparse. There was nothing to rustle and warn of my approach. One corner of the cabin and part of its tarpaper roof peeked through the bushes below. Hunkered low, I started down, chuckling in my throat. This time I would catch Forrest by surprise.

When I could clearly see the round logs notched to fit together at the corner, the circles of growth rings on their cut ends, I stopped. My fire pit sat black and soggy and empty, no black coffeepot, no sign of life. I waited and listened. Maybe he had packed up and gone.

Good. I would have my cabin to myself again, just like I wanted. So how come I felt all hollow inside? I stood up.

"Aiiehh!" Something slammed onto my shoulder. I leaped in the air and spun around yelling, my fists up, ready to fight.

"Hey, Matt! Good to see you." Forrest grinned and held his arms up in self-defense. "I hope you aren't planning to punch me out. I make it a rule never to get into a fight before my morning coffee."

Surprise, relief and anger all hit me at once. I was supposed to sneak up on him, not the other way around. This was all wrong. "How'd you know I was here? I didn't make a sound this time, I know it!"

"I told you, no one can take Forrest by surprise." He glanced away. "A man lives alone long enough, he develops a sixth sense."

I shook my head. "Nah, you must have seen me." Then I noticed, coming from somewhere on the sparsely forested slope behind us, a faint sound of trickling water. That explained everything. He must have climbed up to get water for his coffee. "I bet you were on your way back from the creek and spotted me from above."

Forrest didn't answer, simply walked away. At the cabin door, he stooped to pick up a four-gallon, collapsible water carrier half-filled with murky water. So, I grinned,

I was right, he had been up above. Then the truth hit me.

If he had been coming back from getting water, the jug would be in his hand, not already by the cabin door. Which meant he must have put it down and then circled back around to catch me sneaking up on him. How did he know I was there?

I settled on my log seat and watched him build up the fire. "Can I help?" I asked, but he didn't answer. Was Forrest mad because I didn't believe he had a sixth sense? Just like with Amanda, I had no idea. People were impossible to figure out. This was why I wanted to be a hermit.

I studied the flames crackling around a tent of sticks. One thing I knew for sure was, you can't be a hermit if you have a house-guest. So if Forrest was already mad, now would be a good time to kick him out.

Forrest disappeared into the cabin and returned with his black-as-soot coffeepot. He paused by the water jug to fill it up. "Want some coffee?" He chuckled. "I noticed how much you enjoyed it yesterday."

So, he wasn't angry after all. I grinned and reached for my backpack. "Sure, I'll try some." I pulled out the cream and sugar. "This might help."

He ate four slices of bread slathered in butter and drank two cups of coffee, while I stared into my coffee mug. Once in a while I held my breath and took a swallow. Even with milk and sugar it tasted disgusting.

Finally Forrest threw a last splash of coffee on the ground and stood up. "Ever shoot a crossbow?" he asked.

"No."

"How'd you like to learn?"

I dumped the rest of my coffee out and studied the dying flames, trying to decide what to say. Shooting a crossbow sounded like a sport to me, and I didn't exactly shine at sports. I didn't want to look like a fool in front of Forrest. "I'm not very good at stuff like that," I mumbled.

"I thought you never tried it."

"I haven't, but I can't hit a baseball worth a darn; they kicked me off the soccer team; and don't even ask about hockey."

"So what? Those are kids' games, they don't count for anything. Shooting a crossbow is not a game, it's a livelihood."

"A livelihood?" I glanced up.

"Of course! How do you plan to feed yourself if you can't shoot?"

I hadn't thought that far ahead, I'd always brought food from home.

"Don't worry," he said. "I won't let you shoot yourself in the foot. I've got a foam archery target we can use and a crossbow that's just right for you. We'll set up behind your cabin and see what you can do."

"Okay," I agreed, because I couldn't think of a good excuse.

chapter seven

Thwang! Another arrow found its mark. It hit the target smack in the middle of the bull's-eye. Forrest made it look easy.

Thunk. Another arrow bounced off the cabin wall and dropped uselessly on the ground. Matthew made it look hopeless.

"You're not holding it right," Forrest said. He reached for another arrow. "Here, let me show..."

I lowered the crossbow. "Forget it. What's the point?"

Forrest snorted like an angry bull elk. He waved the arrow in my face, so close I thought he would stick it up my nose. "What's wrong with you?" he bellowed, his blue eyes cold as ice.

My heart thunked into my stomach. That angry face, those awful words, reminded me of my father. A couple of drinks and Dad always started yelling, about the same thing every time. It bugged him that the girl next door could run faster, kick a ball farther and shoot a puck better than me.

Now Forrest had discovered the terrible truth. I tried a lazy smile as if I didn't care what he thought. But when I tried to speak, my voice came out all wrong. I sounded like a hurt little boy. "I tried to tell you, I'm hopeless."

He snatched the crossbow out of my hands. "You're not even trying. Did you listen to one thing I said?"

I turned and walked away, back stiff, eyes burning.

"So," he shouted after me, "is that it? You're giving up, just like that?"

I kept walking.

"You deserve to be a loser!"

I stopped but couldn't turn around. I wanted to yell at him. I wanted to remind him he was staying in my cabin. What kind of a loser did that make him? A grown man with no place to live? But I knew my voice would fall apart if I tried to speak.

His footsteps approached across the mossy ground. "Listen, I'm sorry I yelled, but you've got to try, Matt. How can you learn anything if you give up before you begin?"

I swallowed, the lump in my throat wouldn't go away.

"Matt, if you want to get good at something it takes practice. But I guess you can't be bothered." Forrest strode past me to retrieve the arrows. "I'm out of here."

I opened my mouth to say, Good, I never wanted you here anyway. But a whole different set of words fell out. "You don't have to go, it's my fault..."

He yanked his arrow from the bull's-eye, and then stopped to rub his hand over the join between two logs on the cabin wall. "What I don't get," he said, "is how someone, who put so much time and hard work into this beautiful cabin, won't even try learning something new."

Beautiful cabin. Not childish fort. He was right. I was so afraid of making a fool of myself that I didn't give it an honest try. "Who said I was giving up?"

He glared at me. "Look, Matt, I don't have time for silly games. You said to forget it. You told me you're hopeless. If that means you want to keep trying, then you need to work on your communication skills."

"Okay then, how about this?" I paused, considered and then plunged in. "I made a mistake. I'm sorry. I'd like to try again. Will you please show me how to hit the bull's-eye?"

He threw back his head and laughed. "Bull's-eye? I'd be happy if you get within two feet of the target!"

"Okay." I grinned. "The target it is."

I watched carefully as Forrest took the first shot. His arrow thudded into the target, at the edge of the bull's-eye. I listened to his advice, and paid close attention when he showed me how to hold the crossbow, how to stand, how to aim. Then I raised my crossbow, closed one eye, sighted in on the bull's-eye, pulled the trigger and...Wham! Let it fly.

The arrow shot forward, headed straight for the bull's-eye, slipped down and hit the bottom of the foam target with a satisfying thwang. I threw my arms in the air and shouted like I'd just won a gold medal.

Forrest grinned. "I knew you could do it, Matt!" He handed me another arrow. "Try again. Do what you just did, only better."

"I have to go," I said a few hours later. By then I was slamming into the target every time, from twenty-five yards away. And I hit the bull's-eye more than once. "I can't come up tomorrow because of school, so I guess I won't see you again. Anyway, thanks for the lesson."

"Listen, Matt," Forrest said, "how would you like to go hunting with me?"

"Hunting? Me? When? Won't you be gone by next weekend?"

He rubbed his chin whiskers with his fingers. "Maybe. Maybe not." He dropped his hand and looked at me. "Why don't you take that crossbow home? It's exactly the right size and weight for you. If you practice all week, you might be ready to head out with me next Saturday. But I want you to be accurate from at least thirty-five yards."

"You'll still be here?" Didn't Forrest have a place of his own? Didn't he have a job?

"If you've got my crossbow, I'll have to stay, won't I?" He grinned.

I nodded, but at the same time wondered what he would do up here all week. Still, I was excited at the chance to try hunting. When I was younger and my parents took me hiking we always carried cameras, never crossbows.

Forrest stuffed the crossbow, a cocking aid and four arrows into a cloth sack.

"Wait here," he said and walked away. He returned with something tucked under his arm. Something brown, about two feet high, with four paws and a little white face. "Meet Woody," he said.

I stared down at a life-sized foam wood-chuck perched on its haunches. Its beady little eyes stared up at me. "What's this for?"

"Woody's your target. Practice on him every day, and we'll see if you're ready for the real thing next weekend."

On the last slope of the old logging road, I paused to gaze down at our little town. Lights glowed in the windows of small houses. Beyond them the lake lay steel gray under a darkening sky. I hurried along the paved streets, hoping to get home before Mom. If she saw the crossbow she'd want to know where I got it. Something told me she would never approve of Forrest.

When I saw a light in our kitchen window, I made a quick change in plans and headed through the garage to the basement. My father's workshop was as cluttered as ever. The dry sawdust smell reminded me of better times. We used to build things together. When I was seven we made ten birdhouses in different sizes. We hung them all around the garden.

I held my breath, darted in, stuffed the bulging sack on a shelf and ran back outside. Then I entered the house through the back door.

chapter eight

"Who can name two important things that have contributed to climate change over the last fifty years?" Ms. Petrie asked.

Some of the kids put their hands up, and Ms. Petrie glanced around, searching for a victim. We were supposed to read a whole long, boring chapter about climate change on the weekend. I'm almost sure I took the book home on Friday, so it was probably still in my bag. I bent over to search through the bag near my feet. I pulled out the heavy book along with my science notebook, which I flipped open on my lap.

The room had gone silent around me. A silence that spelled trouble. I risked a quick look, hoping Ms. Petrie's beady little eyes hadn't landed on me. You'd think I'd learn. If you raised your hand, she figured you knew the answer so she left you alone. Sneaky, but it worked every time. She always picked on someone who didn't have a clue.

Ms. Petrie crossed her scrawny arms over her flat chest and said, "Matthew, you're busily studying your notes. Maybe you'd like to start us off? What's one cause of climate change?"

"Uh," I mumbled.

"Pardon me?" Ms. Petrie sauntered toward my desk, her feet huge in flat black shoes that stuck out below a long, shapeless skirt.

I cleared my throat. "Uh," I repeated, a little louder.

Some of the kids laughed. Halfway across the room, Amanda rolled her eyes. She mouthed something, and I knew she was trying to give me the answer. Too bad they don't offer courses in lip-reading at school, now that would be worth taking. Then I'd have four valuable skills: Stop, look, listen, lip-read. I'd be set for life.

Ms. Petrie moved so close I saw every wrinkle around her dark little eyes. Whoa! Talk about a shock! She looked so much like Woody I almost choked. Then her lips parted and she bared her teeth, more like a wolf than a woodchuck. She didn't speak, didn't growl, but she had something green stuck between her front teeth.

Green, I thought. It felt like a clue. I glanced back at Amanda. Her lips were pulled to each side, showing a row of white teeth. I could almost hear the word, *Green*. But then her mouth went round, like an *ow*. Green was not enough. My eyes fell to my notebook to consult my notes: two detailed drawings of my favorite race cars. That's it!

"Cars!" I shouted. "Emissions from cars and trucks create..." From somewhere deep in my brain came my final answer. "Greenhouse gases," I said.

Ms. Petrie showed her teeth again, this time smiling. I leaned closer, trying to decide if it was broccoli or lettuce stuck between them.

"Good, Matthew, I see you've done your homework." Her smile flattened and she went on. "Gases such as carbon dioxide create a greenhouse effect around Earth. They hold heat inside our atmosphere just like the glass of a greenhouse does. And you're right, emissions from gasoline engines create that carbon dioxide."

Amanda winked and flashed me a smile. My eyes flicked back to Ms. Petrie, who loomed over my desk, a frown between her dark eyebrows. I knew she wanted to see my notebook.

Behind her, Tyler spoke up. "Actually, according to the website I consulted, the tar sands are one of the biggest producers of greenhouse gases." He glanced at all the blank faces staring back at him. "That's where they extract crude oil from deep under ground," he explained. "Like in Alberta?"

Ahh—saved by the geek. Tyler might have been the closest thing I had to a friend in this world, but he was still a geek. Ms. Petrie swung around to face him. Tyler sat at the front of the class, his long legs squeezed awkwardly under a desk too small for his tall frame. His messy brown hair curled over thick eyebrows. He loved everything to do with science.

Tyler flicked his hair back and went on quoting numbers and junk he'd learned from some big science website. I picked up my pen and added puffs of dirty exhaust at the backs my beautiful race cars. Then I turned the page and started drawing a crossbow.

After that I sketched a deer half-hidden by bushes. Its big soft eyes looked right at me. Could I shoot it? Did I want to?

"Hey, Matthew!" Tyler's voice made me jump. I looked up to see him and Amanda place their chairs on each side of me and sit down. Amanda dropped her science notebook on my desk, opened it and scribbled something.

That's when I noticed that all the kids had broken into groups of three or four. I sat up straight, shut my notebook and tried to look like I knew what was going on.

"It's so cool we get to work together." Amanda smiled.

"Good choice, Amanda," Tyler agreed. His lips curled up at the corners, the closest he ever came to a smile.

I glanced from one to the other and back again, afraid to say anything that might give me away.

Amanda frowned. "So, are you mad because I chose you and Tyler to work with me on our science report?"

"Uh, no." I cleared my throat. "Of course not. I can hardly wait." I wondered what the report was about.

Tyler rubbed his hands together. "I can pull loads of information from the Internet. I know exactly where I'll go to get started."

No clues there.

Amanda scribbled a note. "We need to

consult books too," she said. "I'll start by going to the library after school."

They both turned to me. Obviously they wanted me to say what I would do to help with the report. I licked my lips and tried to think of something to say, something that would not make me sound like an idiot.

"You don't have a clue what we're talking about, do you?" Amanda asked.

I studied my fingernails. Short, clean and neat.

"Matthew," Amanda said, "why don't you try paying attention once in a while? I thought you'd be all excited about working on this report!"

"Me? Really? Why?"

"Only because it's about the forests you love so much. For your information, we need to do a report on how destruction of forests affects the climate, right here at home as well as around the world."

"Think globally, act locally," Tyler said, dipping his head wisely.

What a geek.

chapter nine

This science report would be a snap, I thought as I walked home from the bus stop. Thanks to Amanda and Tyler, I'd get a good mark and make my mother proud. All I had to do was interview Paul Edwards, the forester who used to be friends with my father. That was Amanda's idea. She said it was important to do research from all different sources and an interview with an expert was the best research tool.

So, okay, I could handle that. Not a problem. I made a mental note to phone him the next day, right after school. I'd make an appointment to meet him and ask my questions. I thought about phoning him as soon as I got home, but the sun was shining and I couldn't wait to get out to the woods.

At home I dropped my schoolbooks near the door, grabbed a snack and clomped down to the basement. I found my father's hockey bag and dumped all his stuff out. It smelled of sweat. It smelled like my father. I held my breath and stuffed his hockey junk into the sack Forrest gave me. Then I put the crossbow and arrows into the hockey bag and laid Woody on top. I rounded up a hammer and some nails, and then I set off.

I walked quickly along the paved streets, glancing this way and that, hoping no one would notice me. Big surprise, no one did. Sometimes I felt like the invisible kid, as if I could walk right into people's houses and no one would see me. Did I blend into the background like a chameleon or did everyone look the other way because they didn't want to see me?

I followed the logging road up and around the first bend. On both sides of the narrow dirt road evergreen trees grew tall and strong. It looked as if the forest went on forever. But I knew better. I ducked off the road and followed a path that cut through the trees. Minutes later I stepped into a clearing that looked like a war zone. As far as I could see, not one tree was still standing. Hundreds of dead trees lay scattered like giant matchsticks tossed on the ground. They crisscrossed over one another and made walking impossible.

Ask a big logging company and they'll tell you clear-cutting is the only way to go. Mow down everything in sight, take the biggest and best trees, and leave the rest lying where they are. Eventually the forest will renew itself. In a hundred years, who's going to know the difference? It's nature's way. That's what they say. But nature doesn't use harvesters, skidders and loaders to destroy a forest. Nature never built roads.

No one but me ever came up here, not even so much as a bird or a squirrel. Why would they? The place was as lifeless as the moon.

I set Woody on a tree stump. Maybe I was wrong, but I was sure the first arrow that hit him would knock him flying, so I hammered some nails through his base into the top of the stump. Then I moved back about twenty-five yards and took aim. My first shot flew out fast and true, the arrow headed straight for Woody's nose. But it swung left, missed him and whooshed into a mess of logs.

I returned to the stump where Woody waited, grinning at me like I was some kind of idiot. Like a mini-Ms. Petrie.

I had no idea where the arrow went. The forest floor lay four feet below a jumble of logs, and the arrow had disappeared somewhere into that mess. I had to get it back. I climbed onto a log and edged along one step at a time, trying to keep my balance on the slippery wet bark. Balancing on a log at the beach is easy. It's not so easy when the log is suspended in midair. My foot slipped. I stopped, caught my balance, and stared down into a rat's nest of twigs and branches. If I fell I might break a leg. I could get stuck and never be seen again. My bones would join the skeletons of these once proud trees.

I gulped, swallowed, took a few more steps and stopped where a dead tree lay across the log I stood on. The tree was thick with brown lifeless branches, impossible to climb over. Beyond it the tangle of criss-crossed logs and branches went on forever. A person could search all day and never find an arrow. For all I knew it had buried itself in the soft dirt below.

I turned around. One arrow gone. I'd have to be more careful.

This time I moved closer to the target, maybe fifteen yards away. If I took my time and remembered what Forrest said, I couldn't miss. I pulled another arrow into place, raised the bow, sighted in on the target and looked at the open spaces all around Woody. My second arrow could fly off anywhere and be lost forever. No, I could do this. Like balancing on a log, if it weren't for the spaces behind, it would be easy. I raised the crossbow, took careful aim and fired. Poor Woody! He took one right in the chest. "That should wipe the grin off your face," I shouted.

After a few more shots I moved back five yards. But already the light was fading, and I could barely see the target. I had wasted most of the daylight, and it was time to head home. Tomorrow, right after school, I'd be up here again.

We didn't have science on Tuesdays, so I didn't have to report on what I'd done so far, which was basically nothing. The minute I walked into the lunchroom, I heard Amanda's laugh. She sat at a big table with friends all around her.

I spotted Tyler at the back of the room, by himself as usual. If I pretended not to see him, he would know something was up because we always sat together. Sometimes we talked a bit, even if we couldn't think of much to say. Mostly we ignored each other and ate our lunches, each thinking our own thoughts, me about the outdoor world and him about the virtual world, I guess.

I walked toward him, carrying my lunch and planning how I would avoid discussing our science report. If they handed out marks for steering conversations away from myself, I'd get an A+ every time.

"Hey, Ty." I dropped into the chair across from him. "What's new in the exciting world of computer games?"

His eyebrows raised in surprise, his mouth full of ham sandwich. He chewed, swallowed and the corners of his lips turned up. "I didn't know you cared," he said. Then he launched into a big explanation of the latest game he was crazy about.

Tyler talked. I munched my lunch, nodded once in a while and thought about target practice. I could hardly wait to get out there again.

chapter ten

The sky was a thick blanket of blackness above my head when I reached town that night. Silver streaks of rain sliced through the streetlights and soaked into my shirt, but I hardly noticed. I was psyched. I hadn't missed the target once, even though I'd moved back to thirty yards. Woody had so many holes he looked like a sponge. Ha! Forrest wouldn't believe it.

Tires swished on wet pavement behind me, headlights swung across our front lawn and chased my long shadow across the grass. Car doors opened and slammed shut. But I kept walking and smiling to myself. If I practiced every day I'd be awesome by Saturday. Forrest would be so impressed he'd take me hunting for sure.

"Hey, Matthew!" Amanda called. "Don't you talk to me anymore?"

I stopped in our driveway, stared at our dark house and thought about running for it. Clutched tightly in my hand, the hockey bag suddenly felt huge. I had to ditch it.

"Matthew?"

Of course I couldn't run away from Amanda. That girl would follow right behind and demand to know what I was doing. I turned around. "Hey, Amanda, I didn't see you in the dark."

I saw her now, though, wearing a hooded jacket to protect her from the rain. "I just got home. My dad picked me up from the library, and I've got stacks of books. Want to come over and help me with our science report?"

"Uh, not now. I have too much to do."

"Oh?" She stepped closer, her face hidden in darkness with the streetlight behind. "Like what?"

Why was she so nosy? She sounded like my mother. "Like help Mom get dinner and do my homework. You know, junk like that."

"Okay. So, did you talk to Mr. Edwards?"

Oops, I'd been in such a hurry after school I completely forgot, but a lie slipped easily to my lips. "Not yet. I tried, but he didn't answer his phone."

"Did you leave a message?"

"Uh, no." Why didn't she just go away and mind her own business? With the streetlight shining on my face Amanda could see me clearly, while she lurked in darkness, a hooded girl without a face.

"I see." She shifted from one foot to the other. "When did you take up hockey?"

"Huh?"

"The hockey bag? Since when do you play?"

"How come you ask so many questions?" I turned away and headed for the house.

Amanda didn't follow, and I didn't feel so psyched anymore.

"Did you hear there was another break-in?" Mom asked. She was slicing tomatoes by the sink. "Everyone at work is talking about it."

I stopped grating cheese for our tacos and turned to face her. "Did they catch the guy this time?"

She shook her head. "No, but I heard the police have a few leads. They think it's someone who lives here, maybe someone new to town."

"Whose place got broken into?"

"Some house at the back of town near the old logging road. And, this time he took canned foods."

"That's all?"

"I don't know, Matthew. The police like to keep it all hush-hush. But I heard a sleeping bag, pillow and tarp were missing too. It makes you wonder if he's some poor homeless person just trying to stay warm and dry."

"I thought homeless people only lived in cities." I went back to grating cheese.

"They can be anywhere, Matthew," Mom said quietly. "And they must get horribly cold at night."

On Wednesday afternoon, I raced home to grab my stuff and head out to practice. I was halfway out the door when I remembered I had to call Paul Edwards. I went back inside, looked up the number and punched it in. The phone rang four times before a voice replied, "You've reached the voice mail of Paul Edwards. Please leave your name and number and I'll get back to you."

His voice sounded so familiar it hit me like a punch in the stomach. Paul and my dad used to be hockey buddies. They hung out together a lot. But after Dad lost his job he stopped playing hockey, dumped all his friends and sat around feeling sorry for himself. I hadn't seen Paul for maybe a year and I couldn't face him now. I started to hang up, but then I heard the beep and decided leaving a message would be easier than talking to him in person. And I had to talk to him soon, or else deal with Amanda and Tyler.

"Uh," I said, in my usual clever way, "this is Matt Henshaw." An image of my father and Paul laughing together settled over me. "Uh," I said again, "Doug's son?" Saying his name brought a sick taste to my mouth. "So anyway, I need to ask some questions about forestry and stuff for school. But I'm going out now so I'll, uh, I'll call you tomorrow."

I slammed down the phone and raced out the door.

On Thursday, Paul answered the phone. "Matthew!" he said, "it's good to hear from you. I understand you have some questions? I'll be glad to help out."

I told him about the report, and we arranged to meet on Saturday afternoon at three thirty. Perfect. I could go hunting early in the morning with Forrest and get to Paul's place in time for the interview.

The minute I walked into the school Friday morning, I knew something was up. Kids crowded around a ninth grade boy named Dylan. This guy was tall and husky, built of muscle from neck to ankle. He always wore a T-shirt that showed off the bulging muscles in his arms.

I spotted Tyler lurking on the edge of the crowd and walked up beside him. "What's up?" I asked.

"Dylan says his house got broken into yesterday," said Tyler.

"What did the Thoughtful Thief take this time?" someone asked.

"Thoughtful Thief?" I whispered to Tyler.

"Yeah. The police call him that because he always removes his boots when he enters someone's house."

Dylan rolled forward on his toes, crossed his arms one over the other to show off his muscles and glared at Tyler and me for daring to talk. "He took my brother's waterproof pants and the jacket he got when he started work last month. And..."

Dylan paused dramatically and surveyed the crowd. "He took some warm sweaters and socks. And..." He paused again.

I felt like walking away from Dylan's little show, but like everyone else I held my breath, kept my eyes on Dylan and waited until he finally added, "The thief broke into our locked freezer and stole some venison."

Big deal. Food and clothes to keep some poor homeless person alive. Hardly worth mentioning if you ask me. I walked away, trying to ignore the little question that had settled at the back of my mind.

chapter eleven

Saturday morning I got up early, made a stack of ham and cheese sandwiches, and grabbed some apples, a few tins of chunky soup and a loaf of bread. I tossed everything into my backpack, and then I picked up a pen to scribble a note.

Hey, Mom,
Gone for the day. Hermit Haven calls!!
See ya later, have fun saling.

I thought for a second, and then I signed my name, *Matt*.

Outside the kitchen window, fuzzy gray fog hung low to the ground and hid the sun. It was the kind of damp cold day that settles right into your bones. I put on my warmest jacket and reached for my father's warm waterproof coat hanging on another peg. He wouldn't be needing it, but Forrest could sure use something to keep him warm.

Mom's footstep in the hall changed my mind in a hurry. I pulled open the basement door, shut it quietly behind me and slipped soundlessly down the stairs. With the hockey bag over my shoulder, I slinked through the garage out into that dull morning.

I had waited all week for this, my first lesson on how to provide food for myself. An important step toward my life's goal.

This time I approached the cabin from a new direction. Wind swished through the treetops to cover any sound from my cat-quiet footsteps. Forrest couldn't possibly hear me coming, not this time. The acrid smell of wood smoke drifted toward me on the breeze. Forrest was awake. I crept closer, parted some tree branches and peered through.

He was crouched by the fire, his back to me, coffee mug in hand. He wore a jacket and pants that looked so warm and new that I was glad I hadn't embarrassed him by bringing my father's old jacket. What was I thinking? Forrest didn't need me. He could take care of himself. For a half second, I wondered where he got the clothes. Then I concentrated on choosing the right moment to surprise him. I would burst out of the bushes and say, Hey, Forrest! What's for breakfast?

Grinning, I pictured his startled leap into the air. He would swing around, surprise all over his face, and his coffee would go flying.

"Are you planning to stand there all day, or come over here and drink your tea?" Forrest called. He didn't even bother to turn around.

My shoulders slumped, and I dragged myself into the clearing. How did he do it? I was ready to believe he really did have a sixth sense, an animal sense. No one could take him by surprise.

Two blackened pots sat over the leaping flames. I moved to the far side of the fire, acting like I hadn't spent the last half hour trying to sneak up on him. "Tea?" I asked, "I thought you only had coffee. Where'd you get the tea?"

He glanced up sharply. "Who said I didn't have tea? If you'd told me you hated coffee instead of pretending to like it, I'd have made you tea last week." He handed me my mug filled with steaming tea. It tasted great.

Thwang! Another arrow found its mark. It landed smack in the middle of the bull's-eye. Matt made it look easy. I grinned at the look of surprise on Forrest's face.

He slapped me on the back. "Way to go, Matt! I'm impressed."

"I practiced every day."

"I believe it. Last Sunday you couldn't hit the side of the cabin."

"Ha! Funny. But seriously, I'm good enough to go hunting now, right?"

His eyes narrowed, and he stared at me as if I'd said something idiotic. "Hunting?"

What, had he forgotten? After all my hard work? A quick prickle of tears stung the backs of my eyes, and I quickly turned away. "That's what you said."

There was a long pause, during which I blinked furiously to get those embarrassing tears under control.

"Well then," Forrest said finally, "if that's what I said, that's what we'll do. But only if you can hit the target ten times in a row from thirty-five yards. I don't want any stray arrows biting me in the butt."

"Not a problem."

Thwang, thwang, thwang. One after the other my arrows slammed into the target. Four out of ten hit the bull's-eye. The other six were close.

"I never would have believed it," Forrest said.

We moved through the forest as silent as wolves. On and on and on we went, hour after hour, up forested hillsides, through mucky ground, across trickling streams and down slippery slopes. Forrest never spoke, never slowed down, never looked back to see if I was still there.

If I stopped for ten seconds, he'd be swallowed up by dense bush, and I'd never find him again. I couldn't ask for a break. He treated me like his equal, and I was determined to prove he was right. But with every step I wished I hadn't swigged two mugs of tea before we set out. I needed to pee. Tea pee.

Forrest stopped so suddenly I almost bumped into him. He raised his hand for silence as I moved up beside him.

He nodded toward a small clearing ahead. I followed his gaze but saw nothing unusual. Forrest didn't move, not even an eyelid, so I didn't either. Then on the far side of the clearing, something moved. I couldn't believe I had missed it before: a huge bull elk, as brown as the tree trunks that sheltered it.

I had seen herds of Roosevelt elk near the roadside, but I had never been so close to one before. This animal, way bigger than a deer, stepped majestically into the clearing, its proud head held high. It sported a rack of branched antlers taller than the height of its body. Round, dark eyes searched warily for any sign of danger. Its nostrils flared as it sniffed the air, but we were downwind where it wouldn't catch our scent. I felt honored to see such a beautiful animal, so wild and so free. It was everything I wanted to be.

Slowly Forrest raised his crossbow. No! He nodded at me. I hesitated for a moment, and then I raised mine too. I held the elk in my sights. Its beautiful head was still raised. This magnificent animal, this symbol of all we have lost. This endangered animal. I pictured my arrow finding its mark, slicing into the elk's brain. I saw the elk's mangled body fall to the ground, blood seeping onto the forest floor. No!

My eyes flicked to Forrest. His hands were steady, his finger on the trigger.

"No!"

chapter twelve

The elk leaped straight up like it was on springs. In one smooth movement it went over the bushes and vanished into the forest.

Forrest swung around, his face twisted with fury. "What's wrong with you, Matt? I spent all day tracking down my game and you scare it away? Are you out of your mind?"

"Uh—" I couldn't speak. This side of Forrest, the way he flew into a rage from one second to the next, took my words away.

"I ought to leave you here. Think you can find your way home?" He turned and stomped away.

"They're endangered!" I called after him. "Here, on Vancouver Island, there aren't many left. You can't kill an endangered animal!"

I couldn't see him but could hear the crash of branches he pushed aside, the crack of twigs under his angry feet.

I ran after him. "Do you even have a hunting license?"

In the next second he was there, huge and fearsome, looming over me. "License?" he shouted. "You think a starving man needs a license to feed himself?"

This time I refused to back down. "How do you plan to get a thousand pounds of elk meat back to the cabin anyway? Even if you could, how are you going to keep it from going bad? Last time I looked, my cabin didn't have a freezer. And besides, how long are you planning to stay?"

Forrest opened his mouth and flapped it shut again. He growled and turned away.

"You're not starving, Forrest!" I yelled. "What about all that canned food? What about the venison?"

He turned slowly, his eyes like ice. "What are you talking about, Matt? You been snooping in the cabin?"

It occurred to me that I hadn't been inside my own cabin since Forrest arrived. "No, but I brought you lots of canned food. And you had venison that first day. Where's the rest of the deer you shot?"

He let out his breath and ran a hand over his whiskers. When he looked at me his blue eyes twinkled. "When you're right, you're right. A man should never take more than he needs. So what do you say we head back to the cabin and heat up some of that soup?"

While we waited for the soup to warm we gobbled down the sandwiches I brought. "I'm sorry I yelled at you, Matt," Forrest said. "Killing that animal would be as wasteful as chopping down an entire forest to take only the prime timber."

"I hate all the clear-cuts up here."

Forrest nodded. "I used to own land. I practiced sustainable logging, milled my own lumber. I was doing all right too. I did my best not to harm the environment."

"What happened?"

"Government changed the rules. I couldn't sell my lumber without paying a huge tax at the border, and I refused to chop everything down to sell only the raw logs. It's not right."

"What happened to your land?"

"I had to sell it when I couldn't afford to pay my taxes. A developer bought it and, guess what?"

"They chopped down all the trees?"

Forrest nodded and reached for the soup pot. "People need to realize they can't keep destroying the environment without paying the consequences," he said.

"Hey, that's what we're studying in science class. I'm supposed to do a report on forests and climate change."

"Then I guess you already know that trees absorb masses of carbon dioxide."

"Yeah. I read something about it," I said.

"Here's something to put in your report: carbon credits."

"What's a carbon credit?"

"Basically, it's buying a license to pollute. So long as they pay someone else not to pollute, companies can go ahead and do all the polluting they want."

We sat by the fire and talked for hours. It turned out being a hermit had not been a lifelong ambition for Forrest. He tried to do his bit to make the world a better place, but when no one listened he gave up.

The minute I reached our driveway that evening the door burst open and Mom ran out. She threw her arms around me, pulling me into the house. The kitchen smelled of melted cheeses, Italian spices and warm garlic bread. My stomach rumbled.

"Matthew! I was about to call the police. Where were you?"

I slipped my backpack from my shoulders, grateful I had left the hockey bag at the cabin. "What's the big deal? Didn't you get my note?"

"Yes, but I didn't think you'd be this late. Matthew, I've been worried sick ever since Paul Edwards called to ask why you didn't show up. What's that about?"

Uh-oh. I completely forgot! "Uh, it's nothing, Mom. I need to interview him for a science report. I'll do it tomorrow."

"Is that the report you're working on with Amanda and Tyler?"

I nodded, wondering how she knew about it.

"Then you're a bit late. Amanda phoned, she and Tyler are coming over tomorrow to get your information and finish up the report."

"Not a problem." My mind raced to find a way out of this one. "I'll phone him tonight. I don't need to see him anyway. I bet he can send all the stuff I need by e-mail."

"Do it right now."

"Can't we eat first? I'm starving."

"How could you be hungry with all the food you've been packing out of here lately?"

Oops, I had really hoped she wouldn't notice. "Uh...I'm a growing boy, right? Besides, I'm stocking up my cabin."

She frowned. "Do you want me to dial the number for you?"

"No, I'll call from my room, that's where my notes are."

I got Paul's answering machine again. "Paul," I said, "it's Matt. Listen, I'm real sorry I didn't meet you today but, uh, something came up. I really hope, if I send you some questions by e-mail, that you can answer them for me? It's really important. Thank you so much!"

chapter thirteen

Someone laughed. Was that Amanda? No, I must have been dreaming. Still tired after that long hike, I turned over and tried to go back to sleep. Faint voices floated down the hall along with an inviting coffee aroma. I pulled a pillow over my head.

Bang, bang, bang. Someone knocked on a door. It sounded far away. Did Mom invite the entire neighborhood over for coffee?

"Matthew! Wake up!" Mom's voice was

muffled. I pushed the pillow away and realized Mom was knocking on my bedroom door. "Matthew, get up! Your friends are here."

Uh.

I flew out of bed, leaped into my clothes, flattened my hair with my hands and ran for the kitchen. If Mom told them I hadn't done the interview yet, they'd take turns strangling me. Even worse, they'd finish the report and leave my name off it. Another big zero for me, as if I wasn't in enough trouble at school already. What a dope! I had a chance to get a good mark for once and I blew it.

"Hi, guys!" I scratched my head and grinned around my fuzzy teeth. I needed to brush them. I needed to pee.

Amanda was sitting at the kitchen table surrounded by books. She looked up and smiled.

"Hey, Matthew!" Tyler leaned his long frame against the counter, his arms folded.

Neither of them looked angry, not yet.

I glanced around. "Where's Mom?"

"Gone jogging," Amanda said. "She was meeting someone."

"Did she say, uh—anything?"

Amanda narrowed her eyes. "You mean, like, 'Good luck with your report. See ya later'?"

"Yeah, whatever. Listen, I need to check my e-mail. Paul was going to send me some stuff. I'll be back in a minute."

I ran to turn the computer on. From there I darted into the bathroom and did what needed to be done. I returned to the computer with an orange toothbrush sticking out of my mouth.

"Please," I whispered, and a fat gob of toothpaste slopped out of my mouth. I caught it in my hand just before it hit the keyboard. Please have the answers for me, I pleaded. Okay, here it comes. Receiving Mail—Twenty new e-mails. Junk, junk, junk, all junk. No, wait, there was one, no two for me.

One was from Tyler, with a ton of attachments: *Got lots of stuff on the forest industry. Don't lose it.*

The other, from Amanda, had one attachment: *C U Sunday at 9. B ready. Report due Monday.*

Monday! I groaned. Tomorrow! I thought it was due next Friday.

"What's up?" Amanda walked into the room with Tyler at her heels.

I moved the toothbrush to the side of my mouth and mumbled around a mouthful of goop. "Nothing. I got your e-mails, but not the one from Paul yet."

"No problem. I've done an outline and organized my notes, and Tyler sent more information than we can use. We just need to add the interview, put everything together, and we'll be done. So, did you tape your interview?"

My eyes flicked from Amanda's face to Tyler's and down to the white goop in the palm of my hand. "Back in a minute." I ran for the bathroom, closed the door and spit in the sink. My face in the mirror was all twisted up. They trusted me and I let them down. What was I going to do now? I rinsed my mouth, drank some water and made up my mind. It was time for me to confess.

"Matthew?" Amanda asked when I returned.

"Uh," I shook my head sadly. "I didn't do it."

"I told you we couldn't trust him," Tyler said in disgust.

A frown creased Amanda's forehead. "Don't be stupid, Tyler. If Matt says he'll get something done, you can count on him."

Ugh. Why did she have to say that? No way could I let her down now. "Uh," I began, and then, out of the blue, inspiration struck. "I meant, I didn't record the interview. Except up here," I pointed to my brain.

"You asked him all the questions we talked about?" Amanda asked. "And you can remember all the answers?"

I grinned. "I have a phonographic memory."

Tyler snorted. "Let's get out of here."

"No, wait, I believe him. Matthew never

forgets anything he hears." Amanda walked over to the computer. "Let's get busy."

I told them what I had learned and Amanda typed my words into the computer. They both fired questions at me, but that was fine because I knew all the answers. Maybe Forrest wasn't the expert they thought I had interviewed, but hey! An expert is an expert, right?

chapter fourteen

For once in my life I handed in a report on time. Maybe Amanda and Tyler had done most of the work, but I did my bit too. The fact that my contribution wasn't quite what it seemed bothered me, but not much.

Three days later when we got our marks, it didn't bother me at all. I couldn't believe it. A big fat A. Matthew Henshaw gets an A in science. Will wonders never cease?

I walked home from the bus with Amanda, and we stopped at the end of her driveway.

She lightly punched my shoulder. "You did good, Matthew. I knew you could if you tried. That was a great interview."

I looked at her smiling face, and the truth rolled smack into the front of my brain. My mouth opened, words formed on my tongue, my eyes widened in horror. What was wrong with me? It was like I'd been slipped a major dose of truth serum and the terrible truth was about to spill out. "Amanda, I didn't..."

"That's weird," she said, staring over my shoulder.

"What?"

"My front door is open." Her eyes swung to my face. "I know Mom locked it this morning when we left."

"I guess she got home early."

Amanda frowned, her face white. "Do you see a car in the carport?"

"No."

"Then no one's home." She marched straight for her front door, which stood open about an inch.

"No! Wait!" I ran after her and grabbed her arm. "Amanda..."

She jerked away. "Let go of me!"

"Are you nuts? What if someone's in there? You can't go barging in. You could get hurt. Come over to my place and call nine-one-one."

She looked at the door and then back at me and nodded.

Ten minutes later two police cars roared into the driveway, lights flashing, sirens screaming. But the thief was long gone.

"We figure he entered the house earlier in the day," one cop told us. "His footprints at the entrance are dry."

"Did he take anything?" Amanda asked.

"That's for you and your parents to tell us."

They wouldn't let anyone in the house until Amanda's mom and dad got home. They wouldn't let me in even then.

When the police finally left, Amanda and her parents came over. Mom had made sandwiches and coffee, but I was the only one who ate.

"What did he take?" I asked. "Food?

Coffee? A roll of toilet paper?" I was almost afraid of the answer.

Her dad looked grim. "He broke the lock on my gun cabinet and made off with my hunting rifle and some ammunition."

Mom leaned her elbows on the table and pressed her fingertips against her forehead. "This is getting scary. He never took weapons before."

I let my breath out slowly. A rifle. Forrest would never steal a hunting rifle. He hated guns. The knot of fear that had been pressing at the back of my brain melted away.

"That's not quite true," Amanda's dad said. "When I noticed my rifle missing, the police let slip about something stolen in the first robbery. They kept it quiet because they didn't want to scare people."

"What was it?" I breathed.

He turned to me. "Two crossbows, an adult's size and a teen's."

I tried to hide the surprise in my eyes and the fear in my belly. Was Forrest behind all this? After school tomorrow I would find out.

chapter fifteen

I couldn't sit still at school that day. My eyes kept wandering to the forested hillsides in the distance. If it weren't such a long bus ride away, I'd have skipped school and headed up to my cabin that morning. After lunch I got a message from Ms. Petrie to come to the science room after school. Not a problem. I'd show up, tell her I needed to be on the bus because Mom couldn't pick me up and be on my way. I wondered what she wanted.

I pushed through the door and my heart stopped. Ms. Petrie sat behind her desk across the room. Seated on one side of her was Paul Edwards. On her other side was my mother. Not one of them looked happy.

"Come on in, Matthew," Ms. Petrie said. "We've been waiting for you."

Right. I just bet they had. Fighting a wave of panic, I glanced back at the open door. Should I run for my life?

"Shut the door, Matthew," my mother said. She knew me too well.

I closed the door and shuffled toward the desk, my eyes fixed on the floor.

"Maybe you can guess why we're here," Ms. Petrie said.

"Uh," I said, which pretty much covered how I felt.

I shifted from one foot to the other and studied my shoelaces. No one said a word. Finally I looked up, under my eyebrows. Ms. Petrie waved the science report at me, the big blue A on top.

"You did an excellent job on this report,"

Ms. Petrie said. "The interview with Paul here made all the difference."

One of my laces had come undone. The ends trailed on the beige floor.

"Paul happens to be an old friend of mine. So when I talked to him last night, I mentioned the report and told him you got an A. I thought he'd be pleased." She paused. "Can you guess what he said?"

My throat seized up. If I said anything now it would only be Uh. So I didn't try.

"Matthew," Mom said, "we're waiting for an answer."

"Uh." I swallowed and looked up. "He might have said I didn't interview him."

Ms. Petrie flipped the pages of the report. "And yet, there are quotes in here from him. How do you suppose that happened?"

What was I supposed to say? This was like a trial. Tried and convicted with three judges and no jury.

Paul spoke for the first time. "I read it and the information is all good. Whoever you spoke to knows what he's talking about. The question is, why lie?"

I couldn't look at him. His eyes would be saying: Like father, like son, you can't trust the Henshaws.

"Who did you get the information from, Matthew?" my mother asked, her voice all squeaky like it gets when she's worried.

I swallowed to keep from saying Uh. If I told them about Forrest, they'd ask more questions, and for sure someone would decide he was the Thoughtful Thief. Mom might figure things out and send the cops up to my cabin. I needed to get up there first.

"Matthew," Ms. Petrie said, "it's time to come clean."

"It was just a guy who used to do sustainable logging. After I missed the interview with Mr. Edwards, I decided to use what he told me."

"What's his name?"

I shrugged. "I don't remember."

"When did you talk to him?" Mom asked.

"I don't know, a long time ago." The lies felt awful, but there was no other way out of this mess. "I remembered what he said, so I went with it. I have a phonographic memory, you know."

After two seconds of surprised silence, all three of them laughed. But not for long. "What you did was wrong, Matthew," Ms. Petrie said, "and I can't give you an A. Don't worry, Tyler and Amanda will still get their marks and, if you cooperate, they don't even need to know what you did. Luckily for you, we came up with the perfect solution."

Great, just what I needed. A teacher/ parent/guy-who-I-lied-about solution.

"What?"

"Paul agreed to an interview for tomorrow, and then you can write a report of your own. If you do a good job, you'll get a passing mark."

"But..." Tomorrow I needed to get up to my cabin.

"You'll do it," my mother insisted, "or be grounded for a month. That means no hikes in the mountains, no visits to your fort."

"Cabin," I corrected.

"Also," she added, "if you don't cooperate

you'll have to tell Amanda and Tyler how you risked their marks by lying."

"That sucks."

"It's your choice."

The interview was set for eleven Saturday, and Mom would drive me to Paul's office. So, if I left the house at dawn I could get up to the cabin and back again in time.

"Are you going to tell me about this man?" Mom asked on the way home.

"There's nothing to tell."

She drove a little farther, and then she said, "Matthew, it's time we talked about what happened."

"I screwed up, okay?"

"No, I mean about your father. He made an unforgivable mistake, and now we're all suffering for it. But you can't keep it inside forever."

A screech of brakes. An ear-splitting crash. I put my hands over my ears. Only the silence of the forest made those sounds go away completely. "I don't want to talk about it."

"Matthew..."

"No!"

chapter sixteen

It was still dark when I reached the logging road. Stars shone close and bright in a cold blue sky. I hiked up the slope feeling weak and dizzy after lying awake all night. I had to do this. I had to talk to Forrest. At the same time, I was afraid of what I might learn.

At my cabin everything was quiet. No fire, no smoke, no sign of life. Good. If he had gone, I wouldn't need to deal with him.

But he might just be sleeping. I crept forward, past the fire pit with its two black pots, up to the battered door. I knocked softly. No answer.

"Forrest?" I called and knocked again.

I pushed the door open and stepped inside. On one side of the dark little room a rumpled sleeping bag lay crookedly on the cot. A rain jacket and pants hung from a nail on the wall. Another nail held a crossbow, the one I had used.

Below the small square window across the room, a board lay across two short rounds cut from a log. The board was loaded with canned food: soups, stews, peaches, coffee and a box of tea bags. Obviously Forrest had not moved out. So, where was he?

On impulse I crossed the room, crouched and peered under the cot. Something was pushed back against the wall. I reached under and pulled out a rifle.

"What are you doing here, Matt?"

From the roots of my hair to the tips of my toenails I went icy cold. Slowly I stood and turned around. Forrest blocked the open doorway, a crossbow in his hand.

"You're the Thoughtful Thief."

He threw back his head and laughed. "Is that what they call me? My father would be proud. He raised me to be considerate of others."

"You broke into people's houses and took their stuff!"

"Look, it goes with the territory, Matt. I don't think of it as stealing so much as borrowing."

"So, you're planning to give everything back?"

"Son, it's a matter of survival. I take only what I need. Those people can afford to replace the stuff I take. Besides, I'm doing the world a favor. I live off the land, don't drive a vehicle, don't use electricity, don't waste water. I'm emissions free! Look at it this way, they're buying carbon credits from me." He grinned.

Maybe he was kidding, but his words only made me angry. "Did your father teach you that too?"

"Did your father teach you to be a hermit?" Forrest snapped.

Screech.

I wanted to cover my ears, but I only clutched the rifle tighter. "Leave my father out of this!"

Forrest pulled off his boots and stepped into the room. "What's up with your dad, Matt? How come you never mention him?"

"Because he's in prison like you should be!" The words flew out and hung in the air like poison. I wanted to snatch them back.

Forrest sank onto the cot, laying the crossbow beside him. "What happened?"

"He drank too much, okay? Drove too fast and hit another car. It was all his fault."

"Anyone hurt?"

"My grandmother was with him." I swallowed, my eyes stung. "She's dead."

Crash.

I couldn't block out his next words.

"You were in the car too."

I nodded.

"That's a tough one, Matt. So, is that why you decided to be a hermit?"

"Maybe."

"Don't care about anyone and you won't get hurt, right?"

"You can't trust people."

"Like me, for example?"

"You lied to me. Now you need to clear out of here."

"Or what, Matt? You'll tell them where I am?"

"They're my friends."

"Hermit's don't have friends."

"Then maybe I'm not a hermit!" I shouted.

Forrest stood up. He seemed to fill the whole room. "If I go, how do I know you won't send the cops after me?"

"Because I said so. I always keep my word." Another lie, but I wished it could be true.

"Why don't you come with me, Matt? I'll teach you how to survive on your own."

"I don't want to."

Forrest twisted his head to one side as if listening to something, and then he started toward me. "Put down that gun, Matt."

Hands shaking, I raised it and backed toward the open door.

"The gun's loaded, Matt. Put it down right now and move away from the door."

"No, it's not yours. I'm taking it with me." I pointed it at him. "Back off!"

"Get away from that door!" he shouted and launched himself at me.

Everything happened in a blur after that. Forrest knocked me down and grabbed the gun from my hands. There was a deafening explosion, and Forrest crashed to the floor. There were shouts from outside, and then several men burst through the door. One of them helped me to my feet. Forrest lay sprawled on the floor, the rifle beside him.

"I killed him!" I screamed.

Then my mother was there, her arms around my shoulders. "No, Matt, the police shot him. They saw him attack you and were forced to take him by surprise."

Blood oozed from Forrest's shoulder and he moaned softly. A police officer pressed on the wound to slow the bleeding.

I knelt beside him. "You're not dead!"

"Not this time, Matt," he whispered. "You okay?"

"Sure, yeah," I said.

He half smiled. "Good. Promise me one thing, Matt. Promise you won't end up like me."

"You'll be fine, Forrest."

"I don't mean promise you won't get shot." He paused, his voice weak. "I mean promise you'll do something better with your life."

When I didn't answer he added, "Don't throw away your own life to punish your dad."

"Whatever."

A police officer knelt down beside me. "We need to get him to a hospital, son," he said.

Forrest looked up, his eyes pleading.

My throat tightened. I couldn't speak.

As they carried him away, only one thought ran through my mind: No one takes Forrest by surprise.

Like *Crossbow*'s main character, Matt, Dayle Campbell Gaetz loves to spend time in the woods. Dayle has written numerous books for young people, including *Spoiled Rotten* in the Orca Currents series, and *Something Suspicious in Saskatchewan*. Dayle lives in Campbell River, British Columbia.

Orca Currents

Pigboy
Vicki Grant

Queen of the Toilet Bowl
Frieda Wishinsky

Rebel's Tag
K.L. Denman

See No Evil
Diane Young

Sewer Rats
Sigmund Brouwer

Spoiled Rotten
Dayle Campbell Gaetz

Sudden Impact
Lesley Choyce

Swiped
Michele Martin Bossley

Wired
Sigmund Brouwer

Visit www.orcabook.com for all Orca titles.